noted
#18/86

SNIPP SNAPP SNURR
LEARN TO SWIM
By MAJ LINDMAN

ALBERT WHITMAN & COMPANY
CHICAGO   ILLINOIS

The Flicka, Ricka, Dicka Books

by MAJ LINDMAN

Flicka, Ricka, Dicka and Their New Skates
Flicka, Ricka, Dicka and the Strawberries
Flicka, Ricka, Dicka and Their New Friend
Flicka, Ricka, Dicka and Their New Dotted Dresses
Flicka, Ricka, Dicka and the Girl Next Door
Flicka, Ricka, Dicka and the Three Kittens
Flicka, Ricka, Dicka and a Little Dog
Flicka, Ricka, Dicka Bake a Cake
Flicka, Ricka, Dicka Go to Market
Flicka, Ricka, Dicka and the Big Red Hen

The Snipp, Snapp, Snurr Books

by MAJ LINDMAN

Snipp, Snapp, Snurr and the Red Shoes
Snipp, Snapp, Snurr and the Gingerbread
Snipp, Snapp, Snurr and the Magic Horse
Snipp, Snapp, Snurr and the Buttered Bread
Snipp, Snapp, Snurr and the Yellow Sled
Snipp, Snapp, Snurr and the Big Surprise
Snipp, Snapp, Snurr and the Big Farm
Snipp, Snapp, Snurr and the Reindeer
Snipp, Snapp, Snurr Learn to Swim
Snipp, Snapp, Snurr and the Seven Dogs

Standard Book Number 8075–7506–2; Library of Congress Card Number 54–9945
© 1954 by Albert Whitman & Company, Chicago
Published simultaneously in Canada by George J. McLeod, Limited, Toronto
Printed in the United States of America
All rights reserved
Third Printing, 1970

Snipp ran up the path toward the cottage.

It was summer in Sweden. Father was going on a long business trip.

Mother was going with him.

She had said, "I feel perfectly safe to let our boys go with Nanny to the seashore.

"She took me to the same little red cottage when I was their age."

On the day they left, Snipp, Snapp, and Snurr went with Nanny to the cottage at the seashore.

They rode the train all morning.

At noon they got off. Up the hill was the little red cottage.

Snipp took his suitcase and ran up the path toward the cottage.

Nanny followed along behind him. Snapp stopped to pick flowers.

Nanny opened the little red cottage and they all went in.

Each boy unpacked his suitcase while Nanny fixed lunch.

The boys took off the clothes they had traveled in, and put on their shorts and sweaters.

After lunch, they ran down the beach to find Nick West and his father. The Wests lived close by and went fishing every day.

Mr. West and Nick were away.

"Of course they are fishing," said Snurr.

"Perhaps not," said Snapp. "The nets are here hanging up to dry."

Nick's cat, Cuddles, walked toward them. Snurr found little fish caught in the nets, and gave them to her to eat.

Snurr gave the cat little fish to eat.

Early the next morning the three little boys went to find the Wests again.

Nick and Mr. West were standing near their boat.

"Hi, boys," Nick called. "We're very glad to see you.

"Hop in with me, all of you. I'm just going out to drop the nets."

Mr. West helped them into the boat. Nick took the oars as Mr. West pushed the boat into the sea.

Snipp and Snapp sat down.

But Snurr began to jump from one side of the boat to the other.

The boat tipped and Snurr fell into the sea.

Nick knew what to do. "Take my oar, Snurr," he said. "Hold on tight and I'll pull you aboard."

"Take my oar, Snurr," he said.

He helped Snurr into the boat. "I have to drop the nets, Snurr," he said, "or I'd take you back.

"You boys should learn to swim if you want to have fun at the sea shore.

"Never jump around in a boat, either. That makes it tip. Now, each of you must sit very still."

Nick rowed out to sea, dropped the nets, and rowed back quickly.

Nanny was frightened when she heard why Snurr was wet from head to foot. And she was cross.

"You boys stay close to me on this beach," she said, "and play with your sailboats.

"I'll do my washing right here where I can watch you. Each one of you should learn to swim."

"You boys stay close to me and play with your sailboats"

When Nanny had done her washing, she hung the clothes on the line to dry.

Her big green tub was empty.

"Let's pretend Nanny's tub is a boat," said Snipp. "Water can't hurt it."

The three little boys pushed and dragged the tub down to the shore.

"Let's push it into the water," said Snurr.

"It will float just like a real boat."

The three little boys gave the tub a strong push that slipped it into the water.

"We're barefoot," said Snapp, "so we can wade in. Let's push it into deep water.

"Climb in with me, Snipp."

The three little boys gave the tub a strong push.

Snipp and Snapp got into the big tub. Snurr stood in the water near them.

There was a light breeze. Behind them was the wide blue sea.

Snapp stood up.

"This is our boat," he cried. "I'm the captain!"

Suddenly the breeze grew strong.

It began to blow the green tub away from shore.

Then Snapp lost his balance and sat down in the tub.

Snipp stood waving his arms and smiling as he said, "Ship Ahoy!"

Snurr stood on the beach.

He watched the make-believe boat floating out to sea.

The strong breeze kept right on blowing.

Then Snapp sat down in the tub.

The two little boys in the tub were now sitting down.

As Snurr watched, he saw that the tub was moving farther and farther out to sea.

Suddenly he knew he could no longer wade out to it.

He called to them, "Hold on. I'll go and get Nanny."

Nanny had just hung her last clean sheet on the line when Snurr ran up to her.

"Oh, Nanny," he shouted. "Snipp and Snapp are floating away!"

Nanny and Snurr ran down to the beach.

When she saw Snipp and Snapp so far away, she exclaimed, "Oh Snurr, whatever can we do?"

Snurr looked at Nanny.

"Oh, Snurr, whatever can we do?"

Then he looked at his two brothers floating farther and farther away.

"Oh, I know, Nanny," Snurr answered. "I will find Nick. I'll run as fast as I can to get him. He'll help us."

Off he ran very fast.

Nick was at home mending his fish nets.

Snurr was out of breath as he ran up. "Nick," he cried, "come with me quickly.

"Snipp and Snapp are floating away in Nanny's green wash tub. We were playing it was a boat."

"Of course I'll come, Snurr," Nick answered.

"I'll get my boat and we'll go after them right now."

Off he ran very fast.

They slid the boat down the beach.

Nick helped Snurr into the boat. He used one oar to push it into the water.

"Stand in the front of the boat," said Nick, "and wave to Snipp and Snapp. They will be very glad to see you. Let's hurry."

Then Nick sat down and began to row with long, even strokes.

Snurr waved to Snipp and Snapp in the tub. "Don't be afraid," he called to them. "We are coming."

Nick and Snurr soon reached the boys. Nick helped them into the boat.

He asked Snapp to hold on to the green tub. Then he rowed them all to shore.

"Don't be frightened!" he called. "We are coming"

Nanny hugged the boys. Then she scolded them.

Nick said, "I want to give them swimming lessons. May they put on their swimming trunks now?"

"Yes," Nanny answered. "I won't ever be happy until you teach them how to swim."

She sent them into the cottage to put on their swimming trunks.

First, Nick showed them how to dog-paddle. They stayed in shallow water close to the beach.

Next, he taught them the breast stroke in shallow water.

He taught them how to dive, and to hold their breath under water.

A few days later he said, "Now you may swim in deep water. Dive off the dock. Don't be afraid."

Nick taught them how to dog-paddle.

All three boys dived in the deep water, then swam back to Nick.

"You boys swim just like three big fish," Nick said proudly.

Nanny said, "What a big surprise you will give Mother and Father when they come to see you."

One fine morning they arrived.

The boys said, "Let's all go for a swim." They could hardly keep their big surprise.

"All right," Mother said. "But keep away from the dock. The water is too deep for you there."

"We're not afraid," said Snapp.

Splash! In went Snipp. Splash! in went Snapp. Splash! In went Snurr. They swam back to shore.

"How wonderful!" said Mother and Father. "What a surprise!"

"Let's all go for a swim"

A week later Father said, "There will be a swimming test for boys today. You may enter it if you like.

"You are to show the judge just how well you can swim."

At two o'clock the boys went with Mother, Father, Nick, and Nanny to a pretty bay of the sea.

Snipp, Snapp, and Snurr started from a point of land in the bay and swam to shore.

Snipp reached the shore first. Next came Snapp, then Snurr and the rest. The judge laid a crown of green leaves on the head of each boy.

It showed they passed the test.

Father said, "Thank you very much, Nick. The boys will never forget their swimming teacher."

Snipp reached the shore first.